Paige!

Merry Christmas!

Ed Paul

THE NIGHT the LIGHTS WENT OUT on CHRISTMAS

ELLIS PAUL

pictures by
SCOTT BRUNDAGE

ALBERT WHITMAN & COMPANY,
CHICAGO, ILLINOIS

This book comes with a FREE song!

Visit www.albertwhitman.com/ellispaul to download the song "The Night the Lights Went Out on Christmas" by Ellis Paul.

This is for Ella and Sofi,
who give me a deeper love for Christmas—EP

For Bonnie,
the night sky's greatest admirer—SB

Library of Congress Cataloging-in-Publication
data is on file with the publisher.

Text copyright © 2015 by Ellis Paul
Pictures copyright © 2015 by Scott Brundage
Published in 2015 by Albert Whitman & Company
ISBN 978-0-8075-4543-0

Printed in China
10 9 8 7 6 5 4 3 2 1 HH 20 19 18 17 16 15

Design by Jordan Kost

For more information about Albert Whitman & Company,
visit our web site at www.albertwhitman.com.

Discover more about Ellis Paul and his music at EllisPaulKids.com.

Every Christmas since 1960, the Johnsons have filled their yard with nifty blinking reindeer, Santas, dwarves, and stars.

CHRISTMAS 1975

It started kind of innocently, just lights within a tree.

Then the mailbox got all lit up,
then the chimney, then the eaves.

Then the half-shell Mary
was blinking neon blue.
Then the hydrant, then the doghouse,
then they built a petting zoo!

With electric livestock—
llamas, horses, donkeys, camels, mules—
and a life-sized baby Jesus,
sparkling like a desert jewel!

Christmas 1983

Well, the lights so rattled the neighborhood
that the Smiths planned a revolt

led by a neon Santa Claus
that buzzed and sparked a thousand jolts.

The Williams rolled out cotton snow.
The Wheelers pinched a grinch.
Mr. Greenberg lit a menorah
with eight foot flames and did not flinch.

The Jacksons inflated snowmen
inside their manger scene.
The three wise men all stood confused.
Snow in the desert? Is this a dream?

Well, things got so darned cluttered
that every house along the street
vanished beneath the twinkling junk,
like pajamas beneath the sheets.

With each new year, this competition gave the families a Christmas mission to see who could outdo themselves with barking penguins, sleighs, and elves.

Pretty soon, from miles around,
people came to Medford Town
to see the sights on Christmas Block,
as lights came on at six o'clock.

The cars, they came in droves and droves,
driving at their leisure.
They'd gawk and squawk and stare in shock,
while their children had near seizures.

Well, even up in outer space,
astronauts could see the place.
The Christmas lights, so bright to see,
made them homesick for their families.

But then one Christmas, it all would change.
There was no space left to arrange,
in all the Johnsons' neighborhood,
except the top where one tree stood.

So Missy Johnson took a star
and, on a ladder leaning far,
she put it on that last tree's top,
and all the neighbors' chins did drop.

Then Jimmy Johnson switched a switch,
Santa's hands turned six o'clock,
and every light in Medford Town
blew out block by block by block.

Then Connecticut, Rhode Island, state by state,
all of America turned black as slate!

O Canada, then Mexico
fell into a deep shadow.

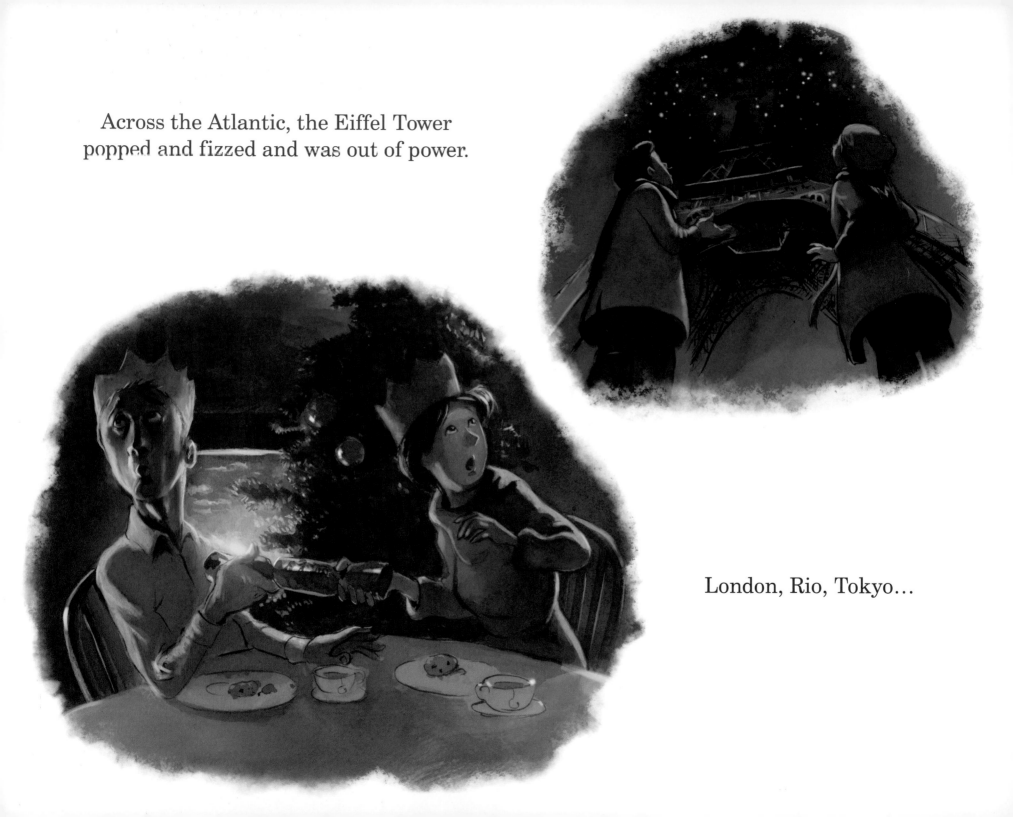

Across the Atlantic, the Eiffel Tower popped and fizzed and was out of power.

London, Rio, Tokyo…

were in the dark (but in the know).

And in this blackout, all did stand,
heartbroken down to every man…

Till Missy Johnson's eyes looked up,
and her little voice did there erupt.

"The stars! The stars! Above our heads!
They've never been so clear!" she said.
And everyone was quite amazed
to see the Milky Way ablaze!

Ten billion stars for every eye
stretched across a newborn sky.
Satellites and meteors—
each were counted by the score.

Now, who would've thought the sky would know
how to put on a Christmas show?
Without that plastic, blinky stuff,
the sky itself was just enough!

See, all it took on Christmas night
to guide three kings was one star's light.
The people stood on Christmas Block
and held on to this simple thought.

Christmas can be neon free
without the snowmen, reindeer, see?
The neighbors, they all sighed relief
'cause those tangled lights can cause such grief.

The next year out on Christmas Block,
they lit a candle on a rock.
They gathered round it merrily.
They sang a Christmas melody.

And no one ever seemed to care
that the decorations weren't even there.

Though maybe they could steal the scene
on the holiday called Halloween.